For information address Disney • Lucasfilm Press,
1101 Flower Street, Glendale, California 91201.

Printed in China
First Hardcover Edition, July 2016   10 9 8 7 6 5 4 3 2 1

ISBN 978-1-4847-8665-9
FAC-023680-16195

Visit the official *Star Wars* website at: www.starwars.com
This book was printed on paper created from a sustainable source.

STAR WARS

AT-AT Attack!

Disney | LUCASFILM
PRESS

Los Angeles • New York

Book Five

Luke Skywalker wasn't always part of the Rebel Alliance defending the galaxy against Darth Vader and the evil Empire. He was raised as a farmer. Now he was fighting with the rebels on a frozen planet called Hoth.

The evil Sith Lord Darth Vader had dispatched thousands of remote probes into the far reaches of space to search for young Skywalker and his allies.

On the frozen surface of Hoth, Luke was riding a tauntaun—
one of the few animals tough enough to survive the intense
cold—when he heard the blast of an Imperial probe. As Luke
went to check out the noise, he was attacked by a vicious beast
called a wampa, which ate his tauntaun. The Jedi used his
lightsaber to escape the beast, but he could not make it through
the dark, brutal cold on his own. He stumbled forward onto the
icy ground.

Barely conscious, Luke heard a familiar voice calling his name.

"Luke," the voice said, echoing in his mind. Luke was weak, but he recognized that voice.

"Ben?" he gasped. It was his teacher, Obi-Wan Kenobi.

Obi-Wan's ghostly image appeared before him. "You will go to the Dagobah system," he said. "There you will learn from Yoda, the Jedi Master who instructed me."

With that, Luke passed out in the snow.

Luke lay in the snow, slowly freezing. Luckily, his friend Han Solo had become worried when the Jedi did not return to the rebel base and had gone out into the cold tundra to find him.

Luke awoke to find himself in the rebel base's infirmary, surrounded by his friends. He was weak, but there wasn't any time to rest. Imperial troops had found them and were approaching the rebel base! Luke quickly put on his pilot suit and left the medical bay. Grabbing his lightsaber, Luke climbed into his snowspeeder.

The Empire had sent giant metal monsters called All Terrain Armored Transports—or AT-AT Walkers—to defeat the Rebels.

Luke and Rogue Squadron attacked the AT-ATs, but their fire bounced right off them!

"That armor's too strong for blasters," Luke said, coming up with a different plan to stop the giant foes.

Luke radioed his fellow pilots: "Go for the legs! It might be our only chance of stopping them."

Luke's team followed his plan, shooting cables around one of the AT-AT's legs and causing it to stumble and fall! One down! The troops inside the rebel base cheered. They might escape after all!

The second AT-AT was soon destroyed, but so was most of Rogue Squadron. Luke was one of the last pilots left. He needed to take down the final walker.

Just as Luke circled around for another attack, the rebels realized that Darth Vader had entered the base! Han Solo pulled Princess Leia aside. "Come on," he said. "That's it." It was time for them to go.

Leia turned to her last soldiers and told them to get off Hoth safely.

Han, Chewbacca, C-3PO, and Princess Leia boarded Han's ship, the *Millennium Falcon*. Han knew they would make it . . . as long as Luke stopped that last AT-AT outside!

They couldn't wait any longer. "Punch it!" Han shouted to Chewie. The *Millennium Falcon*'s engines roared to life, and the ship darted toward the exit!

As Luke flew toward the AT-AT, his snowspeeder was hit. He was going down!

Luke struggled to eject. He jumped into the snow just as the AT-AT's giant foot stomped on the vehicle. With his snowspeeder destroyed and no blaster powerful enough to pierce the walker's armor, all Luke had left was a grappling hook, a grenade, and . . . his lightsaber. But what could a lightsaber possibly do against an AT-AT?

Luke picked himself up out of the snow and concentrated. He used the Force to help him run more quickly than he ever had before and caught up with the AT-AT. Firing his grappling hook at the underside of the walker, he used it to pull himself up to the belly of the beast!

Luke wondered how he would get through the mechanical monster's tough armor. Then he remembered the first thing Obi-Wan had ever told him about a lightsaber: "This is the weapon of a Jedi Knight. An elegant weapon for a more civilized age." At the time, he'd had no idea how much that lightsaber would change his life.

Luke ignited his lightsaber and slashed through the AT-AT's armor, creating a hole in its belly. He threw a grenade into the opening and then quickly dropped back into the snow!

Exhausted from the effort, Luke waited for the . . . *BOOM!*

The AT-AT exploded, crumpling to the ground. He'd done it!

Luke watched as the *Millennium Falcon* zoomed past him and into outer space. He was happy to know that his friends were all safely aboard.

Darth Vader was outraged that the rebels had escaped. But there would be another time and another fight. Darth Vader was as patient as he was deadly.

Luke looked down at the lightsaber in his hand and realized that the weapon of the Jedi Knights had saved his life again.

With the AT-ATs' attack thwarted and his friends headed away from Hoth in the *Millennium Falcon*, it was time for Luke to choose between becoming a soldier and becoming a Jedi Knight.

Luke knew that the power of the Jedi had saved them that day. He remembered that Obi-Wan Kenobi had appeared to him—had he been a ghost?—and told him to find the powerful Jedi Master, Yoda. With that last thought in his mind, Luke set his course for the Dagobah system. He was ready to become a true Jedi Knight.